Glock around the clock

Simple ideas for tuned percussion in the classroom

By Jane Sebba

Illustrated by Alison Dexter

A & C Black • London

First published 1997
A & C Black (Publishers) Ltd
35 Bedford Row London WC1R 4JH
© 1997 A & C Black (Publishers) Ltd

Book/cassette pack ISBN 0-7136-4635-7
Book/CD pack ISBN 0-7136-4636-5

Written by Jane Sebba
Edited by Ana Sanderson
Text © 1997 A & C Black
Illustrated by Alison Dexter
Designed by Dorothy Moir
Printed in Great Britain by St Edmundsbury Press Ltd,
Bury St Edmunds, Suffolk

Recording presented by Jonathan Trueman
Songs performed by Helen Speirs
Other performers: Jane Sebba and Ana Sanderson
Recorded and mastered by Darren Nicholls
74 minutes playing time

Contents

CHORD ACCOMPANIMENTS

COMPOSING ACTIVITIES

About this book

We have all yet to meet a child who hasn't been instantly intrigued and delighted by a classroom glockenspiel. The instrument is child-sized and easy to handle, a pleasing sound can be produced immediately, and its versatility ensures that no-one gets bored.

However, the task for the teacher of organising several children at once to participate in a tuned percussion activity can be daunting – often leading the teacher to feel despondent about tuned percussion and how to use it in the classroom. The purpose of **Glock around the clock** is to make playing tuned percussion instruments instantly accessible. Without reading a note of music, you can give your children a tuneful and educational musical experience which both you and they will enjoy.

All children sing, some more tunefully than others, but whatever their vocal skills, they cannot see the mechanism which creates the sound. However, tuned percussion instruments, with note-bars arranged so neatly and satisfactorily, provide us with a perfect visual aid for teaching our children about pitch in music. With the name of the note marked on each bar, and the size and position of each note clearly visible, even children who find abstract concepts hard to grasp will understand the principles of high and low.

Finding your way around the book and recording

There are three sections in the book: **musical games** (pages 8 – 23), **chord accompaniments** with well-known songs (pages 24 – 41) and **composing activities** (pages 42 – 59). The items in each section progress from easy to more difficult. You can work through a section to give your children the opportunity to accumulate musical skills; alternatively, you can pick and choose items suitable for your children. Some items can be used as quick warming-up activities, while others can last for one or more lessons.

Nearly all the activities can take place in the classroom. Many take into consideration limited resources and require only one instrument. Others give ideas for using more instruments if you have them.

The accompanying recording takes you step-by-step through all the activities, giving you the opportunity to hear how the musical games might progress, how the songs and their chord accompaniments should sound, and example compositions which might result from the items in the composing activities section. If you are a confident musician, this book will provide you with a wealth of new ideas; if you are not, it will guide you gently into practical music-making.

Classroom music-making

Your music lessons incorporating percussion instruments will be enjoyable and productive if both you and your children observe the following points.

Successful music–making is often a product of good team–work.

Just as football players must be aware of the other members of the team, so must musicians be aware of and listen to others in order to play together as a team. Listening to others is a skill in its own right and some children will find it difficult at first. Point out that playing a musical piece is not a race or competition to win or to be the first to finish.

Establish some ground rules for when to be silent.
When you give a child a percussion instrument, (s)he will want to play it – and the effect is often noisy! It is very difficult to give instructions for a musical performance when several children are playing percussion instruments, so it is advisable to make a rule that instruments and beaters should be placed on the floor or a table when not in use.

Silence is an important component of music. Encourage the performers to be still like statues at the beginning and at the end of their pieces. Listeners should always be quiet while others perform – and performers should give their audience something worth being quiet for!

For each item in this book which includes a song, starting notes for the tune are given.
When combining singing with tuned percussion, it is important to begin singing on the correct note. To find your starting note, you can either

familiarise yourself with the recording, or you can play the first note given in the **teacher's help box** on a tuned percussion instrument, and then reproduce it vocally. The **teacher's help box** below shows a song beginning on the note **D**.

The alto xylophone is closest in range to children's voices, so if you have one, use it for giving starting notes. If you find it difficult to reproduce notes vocally, delegate the job to someone in your class for whom it is easy.

For each item which includes a song or a chant, a pulse should be established so that everyone performs at the same speed.
You can take the pulse from the relevant track on the recording. Alternatively, you can look at the count-in given in the **teacher's help box**, take a moment to establish the speed of the song or chant in your head, then count aloud to bring everyone in together. Tell the children beforehand what you are going to count and when they should start singing. The **teacher's help boxes** below show a song and a chant, both with four beat count-ins. The circles above the words of the chant indicate the pulse.

Teacher's help box:
showing count-in, beat and first notes of the song

Teacher's help box:
showing count-in and pulse of the chant

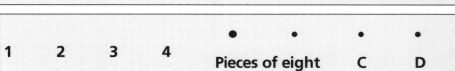

1	2	3	4	1	2	3	4
				D	D	A	A A
				Lis - ten	care - ful - ly

1	2	3	4	•	•	•	•
				Pieces of eight	C	D

Tuned percussion instruments

The tuned percussion instruments referred to in this book are the most commonly used ones – xylophones, glockenspiels, metallophones and chime bars. When the note-bars of these instruments are struck, a definite pitch or note (such as **A**, **B** or **C** and so on) is heard. By contrast, untuned percussion instruments (such as tambourines, drums and cymbals) produce sounds which have no definite pitch. On a tuned instrument, you can literally play a tune. Try playing the beginning of *Frère Jacques* – **C D E C C D E C**.

Recognising different tuned percussion instruments

In Greek, *xulon* means wood, and *phonos* means sound, giving us the word xylophone. Xylophones have wooden bars which rest on a deep resonator box which helps to amplify the sound.

In German, *glocken* means bell, and *spiel* means play, giving us the word glockenspiel. Glockenspiels have shiny metal bars which are usually thin and narrow. They are often black and white, as on a piano. The sound of the glockenspiel is bell-like.

Metallophones also have metal bars, but they are thicker and wider than those of the glockenspiel. They are made of a metal alloy with a matt finish. Like the xylophone, the bars rest on a deep resonator box.

A chime bar is a single bar, made out of wood, fibre or metal, mounted on its own small resonating box. Each chime bar can sound one note only. Chime bars can be purchased individually, or as whole sets - a set can be played in the same way as a xylophone, glockenspiel, or metallophone.

Family members

Glockenspiels, xylophones, metallophones and chime bar sets are available in different sizes. The smallest instruments produce the highest notes and are called soprano instruments; the largest in size produce the lowest sounds and are called bass (pronounced base) instruments; the instruments in between, both in size and sound, are the alto instruments.

The notes and their names

Most instruments will have at least one row of twelve note-bars. Place the instrument with the longest bar which produces the lowest note to the player's left. The shortest bar which produces the highest note should be to the player's right, so that from left to right, the sound of the instrument gets higher.

The musical note names – **A B C D E F G** – are the first seven letters of the alphabet. There is no H; after **G**, the sequence of letters repeats. The result is that there are several notes of the same name related to each other by their sound as well as their name. If you play a high **D** and a low **D**, you will hear that they are the 'same' note. In this book, high notes, such as high **D** are shown as **D'**. Low **B** is shown as **B,**.

Diatonic and chromatic instruments – sharps and flats

Diatonic tuned percussion instruments have only one row of notes which correspond to the white notes on a piano. A chromatic tuned percussion instrument has a second row of notes which corresponds to the black notes on a piano. These are the sharp (♯) and flat (♭) notes. A sharp note sounds a little higher than its namesake, (**F♯** is higher than **F**) and a flat note sounds a little lower, (**G♭** is lower than **G**). Each note on the second row of the instrument has two names – one sharp and one flat. **G♭** and **F♯** are the same note. Each note on the second row is generally labelled with its more commonly used name. **F♯** is more commonly referred to than **G♭**.

Beaters
There are many different types of beaters; hard (wood or plastic), medium-hard (rubber or medium-hard plastic), hard felt and soft felt. Beaters can also differ in size and weight; a better sound quality can be achieved with heavier beaters. The sounds produced on tuned percussion instruments will vary according to the type of beaters used to play them. Children will enjoy experimenting with hard and soft heads on all the instruments. Any beater can be used to play any instrument, with the exception of hard beaters on metallophones, as they can damage the metal alloy.

Holding beaters and space to play
If you have sufficient beaters, give each child a pair of identical beaters, one to hold in each hand. Your children will probably prefer to use their dominant hand, but encourage them to alternate their hands.

The note-bar should be struck with the round head of the beater. The other end should be held in the palm of the hand, with the fingers lightly wrapped around the stick and the back of the hand facing up. The beater should not be held as though it were a pencil. The wrist must be flexible, to enable the head of the beater to bounce gently off the bar. Some children may need frequent reminders about how to hold the beater.

To achieve a good sound quality from a tuned percussion instrument, the head of the beater should 'bounce' off the bar. The children can imagine that the head of the beater is a ball, and bounce it gently off the centre of the bar, between the two rows of pins. This enables the bar to vibrate freely, and allows the instrument to resonate. If the head of the beater remains on the bar, the vibration is dampened, and the sound will 'die'. Some children find this action difficult and will need to practise.

Make sure each player has plenty of space. Ideally, instruments should be at a child's waist level on a table so that the children can stand to play. If instruments are placed on the floor, encourage the children to kneel to play so that their arm movements are not restricted.

Making tuned percussion parts easier to play
To help children see which note-bars they should be using for a particular activity or song, you can either highlight the note-bars by placing stickers on them, or remove those not being used. Bars on xylophones, glockenspiels and metallophones can be removed easily – simply ensure that they are lifted off the instrument with both hands. (Never lever them up at one end.) Always replace all bars correctly after a session.

For information about classroom percussion instruments, read *Agogo bells to Xylophone* (see back cover).

In this game, the children sort out the jumbled notes of the scale of **C** major into order from lowest to highest, by listening.

You will need:
• these eight chime bars (which are the notes of the scale of **C** major)

• eight beaters
• a large piece of material or paper.

Mary should go to the beginning of the line

Winston should play last

Latoya should play second last

Micky should play second

Mahesh should play sixth

The game

1. Everyone listens to the eight chime bars played in order from lowest to highest.

This is the order into which the children will organise the notes.

2. Muddle up the chime bars.

Place them underneath the piece of material.

Allocate the beaters to eight children – the players. Ask them each to take a chime bar from under the material, keeping it hidden from the children in the circle. These eight children now stand in a line.

3. The players strike their notes one at a time.

They play in the order of their line, from left to right as the rest of the children see them. The notes will (almost certainly) not be ordered from lowest to highest.

4. The listeners sort out the notes into order, from lowest to highest.

They listen to the chime bars in turn and tell the players to move position to order the notes. This may require several instructions. After each instruction, listen to the new order.

This process is continued until the notes are played in the correct order.

Variations

- Ask the sorters to order the notes from highest to lowest.
- Use the notes of a minor scale, such as C minor: **C D E♭** (also called **D♯**) **F G A♭** (also called **G♯**) **B C'**.

(Pirates chant)

Pieces of eight C D

Pieces of eight E F

Pieces of eight G A

Pieces of eight B C

Pretty Polly,

We've been told,

You know where

To find the gold.

(Parrot plays)

C D E F G A B C'

This game focusses on dynamics (volume). Some imaginary treasure is hidden in an imaginary chest which can be opened with a magic letter – a note name. One child (the *parrot*) communicates the magic letter to the other children (the *pirates*) by playing the corresponding note with a contrasting dynamic while performing the whole scale of **C** major.

You will need:
• a tuned percussion instrument with these notes for the *parrot*

• any other tuned percussion instruments containing all these notes, or pairs of them, for the *pirates*.

1	2	3	4	•	•	•	•
				Pieces of eight		**C**	**D**

The game

1. Prepare for the game.
Choose a child to be the *parrot*. (S)he sits by the instrument. The rest of the children are *pirates*. Allocate any spare tuned instruments to them.

2. The pirates *perform their chant.*
As they say each letter at the end of the first four lines (**C**, **D** and so on), some *pirates* can join in playing the corresponding notes.

3. The parrot *plays a clue for the magic letter.*
After the chant, the *parrot* plays the scale loudly or quietly. However, the note corresponding to the magic letter should be played at a contrasting volume to the other notes.

4. The pirates *listen and work out which note was played at a contrasting dynamic.*
The first *pirate* to deduce correctly the magic letter becomes the new *parrot*.

Variations

- Position the *parrot* and his/her instrument so that the *pirates* cannot see him/her.
- Perform the chant, reversing the order of the notes: *Pieces of eight* **C' B** ...
- Ask a group of *parrots* to communicate a magic word made up of some of the seven note names, eg DAB, DEAF, BADGE, DECADE, CABBAGE. The *pirates* chant, a *parrot* gives a clue for the first letter, the *pirates* chant, another *parrot* gives a clue for the second letter, and so on.

Photocopiable minute cards

In this game, the children tell what the time is by listening to musical clues played by two children – a *minutes player* and an *hour player*.

For each small group, you will need:
- these notes for the *minutes player*

- this note for the *hour player*

- a set of *hour cards*
- a set of *minute cards*
- several clock faces
- pencils.

Photocopiable hour cards

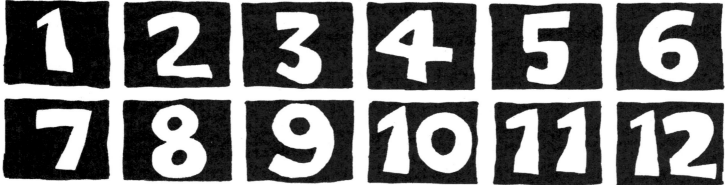

The game

1. Familiarise the children with the minutes tunes.

Play the tunes on four different minute cards:
- the four note tune indicates 'quarter past';
- the eight note tune indicates 'half past';
- the twelve note tune indicates forty-five minutes past the hour – in other words, 'quarter to' the next hour;
- the sixteen note tune indicates 'o'clock'.

Give the children an opportunity to practise playing the tunes.

2. Divide the children into small groups.

Give each group instruments, sets of photocopied cards, shuffled and placed face down, and several clock faces.

3. A minutes player and an hour player perform.

Choose a minutes player and an hour player. They turn over a card each. The rest of the children listen as the players perform the minutes tune and number of chimes corresponding to the hour.

4. The listeners tell the time.

Each listener takes a clock face, draws on hands and writes the time.
Repeat the game with different players.

Photocopiable clock face

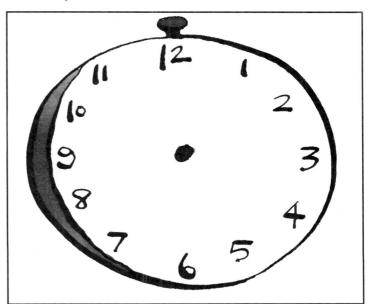

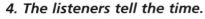

This material is photocopiable for the teaching purposes specified in this book.

Chorus chant
What are you wearing? Dungarees or skirt,
Stripes or spots or a plain white shirt?

Sample verses
  What are you wearing?
    Black shoes.
  What are you wearing?
    Black shoes.

What are you wearing?
  An earring in each ear.
What are you wearing?
  An earring in each ear.

What are you wearing?
  A long-sleeved shirt with stripes on it.
What are you wearing?
  A long-sleeved shirt with stripes on it.

In this activity, the children think of items of clothing and make tunes which move up and down by step, ending on a high **C** or a low **C**.

You will need:
• an instrument with these notes and two beaters for the verse answers

• one enlarged photocopy of the question opposite
• one enlarged photocopy of the numbered instrument chart opposite
• (optional) an instrument with these notes for the verse question.

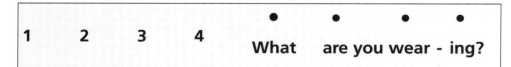

The game

1. Teach the chorus chant and the verse question 'What are you wearing?'

Say the words of the chorus chant rhythmically. The children can sing (and play) the verse question; the tune is shown here.

2. Each child suggests an answer in a performance of the chorus and verse.

Each answer can have up to eight syllables. Repeat the chorus and verse as necessary.

3. Each child works out two tunes, one rising and one falling, to fit his/her answer.

The musical phrases must follow these rules:
• There should be one note per syllable;
• One phrase moves up by step, ending on high **C**; the other moves down by step ending on low **C**.

The children work out on which notes their phrases should begin in order to end on the correct notes. To help them, show an enlarged photocopy of the numbered instrument chart.

4. The children incorporate their musical answers into a performance.

The children sit in a circle. Position an instrument in front of the first child performing an answer. (If you wish, position another instrument in front of another child opposite to play the verse question.)

All the children perform the chant and sing the verse question. Then the child with the instrument performs a rising answer. The children sing the verse question again; this is followed with a falling answer. As the children repeat the chant, the instrument is passed on to the next child in the circle. Continue until everyone has had a turn.

Verse question – tune

G	E	A	G		E
What	are	you	wear	-	ing?

Numbered instrument chart

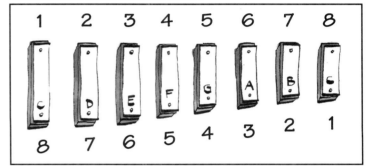

Sample answer phrases

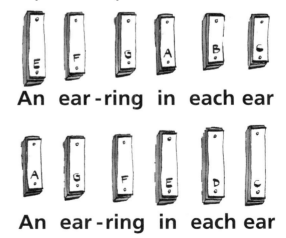

An ear-ring in each ear

An ear-ring in each ear

This material is photocopiable for the teaching purposes specified in this book.

I went to market and I bought
an armadillo *(play)* A, A, A, A,

I went to market and I bought
an armadillo *(play)* A, A, A, A,
and a biscuit *(play)* B, B,

... I went to market and I bought
an armadillo *(play)* A, A, A, A,
and a biscuit *(play)* B, B,
and a catapult *(play)* C C C and a
dog *(play)* D and an egg *(play)* E
and a feather *(play)* F F
and a generator *(play)* G G G G
and an apple pie *(play)* A A A

I don't like apple pie *(play)* A A A
so I gave that back, but I kept the generator *(play)* G G G G
and the feather *(play)* F F ... and the armadillo *(play)* A, A, A, A,

I don't like generators *(play)* G G G G
so I gave that back, but I kept the feather *(play)* F F and the
egg *(play)* E ... and the armadillo *(play)* A, A, A, A,

I don't like armadillos *(play)* A, A, A, A,
so I gave that back, but I went to market and I bought
an anklet *(play)* A, A,

In this musical version of the game *I went to market and I bought an apple*, the children think of words beginning with the note names **A B C D E F** and **G**. They play the rhythms of the words on the notes.

You will need:
• one instrument with these notes.

The game

1. Prepare for the game.
Place the instrument on a table. The children stand in a circle around the table.

2. A child stands by the instrument.
(S)he begins by saying 'I went to market ...' and chooses a word beginning with the letter A for the list. (S)he plays its rhythm on the note A_1.

3. The next two children perform.
One chooses a new word beginning with B and plays its rhythm on B_1. The other then performs the word beginning with A on A_1.

4. The next three children perform and the pattern is continued.
The children continue adding and playing new words beginning with the remaining letters C D E F G and A.

5. The children begin a new pattern.
The next child says 'I don't like ...', and says and plays the rhythm of the word thought of by the previous child. The rest of the words are then said and performed in reverse order by the next children (the notes going down instead of up).

Continue until it is time to begin the first pattern again.

Variations

- State new words but do not repeat them. Just play their rhythms on the respective notes.
- Children can join in with words being played, either by singing or by playing any available untuned percussion instruments.

This musical version of *Simon says* uses two different pairs of notes – **D** and **F♯** (a major third) and **D** and **F** (a minor third). In the musical version of the game, the major third replaces the instruction 'do this' and the minor third replaces the instruction 'do that'.

Major and minor thirds are two examples of **intervals**. Interval is the musical term for distance in sound between two notes.

You will need:
• these notes

• two beaters.

The game

1. Familiarise the children with the sounds of the intervals.
Before playing the game, the children must be familiar with the sounds of the intervals to be used in the musical version of the game. Play the notes making each interval one at a time, naming the interval (major third or minor third).

2. Play **Wendy whispers** using the words 'do this' and 'do that'.

Whisper 'do this' and perform an action.
The children copy your action.

Whisper 'do this' and perform an action.
The children copy your action.

Whisper 'do that' and perform an action.
The children remain still.

3. *Play* Wendy whispers *using the intervals.*

The major third replaces the instructions 'do this' and the minor third replaces the instruction 'do that'. Play **D** then **F♯** for the major third, and **D** then **F** for the minor third.

Play **D** then **F♯** and perform an action.
The children copy your action.

Play **D** then **F♯** and perform an action.
The children copy your action.

Play **D** then **F** and perform an action.
The children remain still.

Variations

• Play the notes of each interval simultaneously.
• Play the game using the notes **D** and **B** (a major sixth) and **D** and **B♭** (a minor sixth)

Remember to familiarise the children with the sounds of the intervals before playing the game.

(1st version)

Bank raid *(click, click)*
   Hot on the trail *(click, click)*
Bank raid *(click, click)*
   Close on your tail *(click, click).*

(2nd version)

Bank raid *(note, note)*
   Hot on the trail *(note, note)*
Bank raid *(note, note)*
   Close on your tail *(note, note)*

In this game, there are opportunities for inventing, copying, conducting to indicate dynamics (volume) and performing sound effects at appropriate dynamics.

You will need:
• two instruments with these notes (use identical instruments if possible)
• three cards made from photocopies of the pictures below.

Chief of police

Robber

Cop

This material is photocopiable for the teaching purposes specified in this book.

1	2	3	4	●	●	●	●

Bank raid *(click, click)*

The game

1. Perform the first version of the chant.
The children sit in a circle with the instruments placed in the centre. While the chant is performed with tongue (or finger) clicks, the cards are passed separately around the circle.

At the end of the first version of the chant, the children with the *robber* and the *cop* cards go to the instruments. The *chief of police* stands up.

2. The child with the chief of police card conducts the rest of the children making police car sounds.
The *Chief of police* moves his/her hands together and apart to indicate whether the cars begin far away (quiet) and come closer (get louder) or the opposite.

3. Perform the second version of the chant.
This time, there are no finger clicks. Instead, after the first and third lines of the chant, the *robber* plays a made up two note pattern (the same pattern each time). After the second and fourth lines, the *cop* copies the *robber's* pattern.

The teacher, who is the *judge*, announces whether or not the *robber* was 'caught' (correctly copied).

4. The game is repeated with a new chief of police, robber and cop.

Variations
• Position the *robber's* instrument so that it cannot be seen by the *cop*.
• The *robber* plays different patterns at the end of the first and third lines.
• Play the game with three other notes, such as **D**, **G** and **C'**.

Franz Liszt
Claude Debussy
Ralph Vaughan Williams
Johann Sebastian Bach

Blue shoes
That's delightful
Call an ambulance
Tasting deliciously sweet

George Gershwin
Benjamin Britten
Claudio Monteverdi
Wolfgang Amadeus Mozart

Start writing
Recycled paper
Excellent education
Watching television programmes

Edvard Grieg
Bela Bartok
Ludwig van Beethoven
Peter Ilyich Tchaikovsky

Going home
Sloppy slippers
Doing the minimum
Peeling yellow bananas

This material is photocopiable for the teaching purposes specified in this book.

In this game, the children play rhythms using the notes which make up major and minor chords.

Some children play the rhythms of the names of four Western classical composers using the notes of the major and minor chords. The rest of the children listen to identify which composers' names are played. (If you prefer, you can play this game with the alternative phrases suggested, which have rhythms matching the composers' names.)

You will need:
• two tuned percussion instruments, one with the notes of an **F** major chord:

and one with the notes of a **D** minor chord:

• photocopies of a group of composers' names or phrases
• pencils and paper.

The game

1. Familiarise the children with the names of a group of four composers.

Choose a group of four composers. The children need to be familiar with both how the composers' names sound and how they are written. (You can hear the pronunciation of all the composers' names on the accompanying recording.)

2. Choose four children to play the rhythms of the composers' names.

Silently allocate a composer's name to each player.

Each child plays the rhythm of his/her composer's name on a tuned percussion instrument, using the notes of either the **F** major or **D** minor chord. Each player can start on any note of either chord and play notes in any order.

3. The rest of the children listen to work out which composers' names are being performed.

The children may need to hear the rhythms played several times in order to work them out. It may help to clap each rhythm after it has been played.

The children write down who they think is playing each name or phrase and reveal their answers when all of the players have performed.

Variation

- Play the game using names, words or phrases suggested by the children.

Help with chord accompaniments

Chords and chord accompaniments
Two or more notes played at the same time make a chord. In this section, the children play chord accompaniments by performing three instrumental parts simultaneously with a song.

Counting the beat
Each song has a steady beat which the children must be aware of in order to perform the chord accompaniments. Divide the children into two groups, one to sing the song and the other to count the beat; this way, everyone can hear how the count fits with the song.

Preparing to play a chord accompaniment
It is difficult to sing and play an instrumental part at the same time, so divide the children into singers and players, and then swap roles. The instructions in this section take you and your children through simple preparation leading to a successful performance at the end. Remember to establish a steady beat before you start to sing, and keep the speed steady throughout the song. The recording which accompanies this book demonstrates how to do this with each track.

The teacher's help box

The count in
The steady count continues throughout the song. The children play their notes on the circled counts – in this case, the first counts.

The melody notes and lyrics of the first line
These are shown above the steady count. Be sure to start singing the song on the right note (in this case the note **D**).

		D	D	B, D	G	A	B	B	B	A	G	
		John	Brown's	bro-ther ran	from here	to Tim - buc -tu						
1		2	①	2	①	2	①	2	①	2
1st part		D		D		D		D	
2nd part		B		B		B		B	
3rd part		G		G		G		G	

The instrumental parts
These are labelled and the first line of each instrumental part given. (Read across to see the notes.) In this song, the first line of the 1st instrumental part consists of the note **D** played four times.

The chords
By reading vertically, you can see what happens simultaneously. For example, on the first (circled) beat after the count in, the word 'John' is sung on the note **D**. At the same time, the first notes of all of the three instrumental parts (**D**, **B** and **G**) are played, making a chord.

24

The pupils' instrumental parts

Instrumental part
Though labelled 1st, 2nd and 3rd parts, the instrumental parts are all equally important.

The count
The children need to be aware of the steady beat throughout the song. The children practise counting th beat (1 2 throughout in this case) before learning the instrumental parts.

When to play
The notes of an instrumental part are played on the circled beats, in this case the 1st beats, not the 2nd beats.

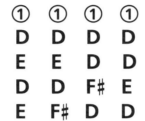

John Brown's brother

1st part (D E F♯)

**Count 1 2 throughout
Play on ① (the 1st beats)**

①	①	①	①
D	D	D	D
E	E	D	D
D	D	F♯	E
E	F♯	D	D

Play twice; once for the verse and once for the chorus.

The notes needed
The two, three or four notes required for an instrumental part are specified here.

Reading the notes
Each line of notes is read separately. The notes are played one at a time.

Additional instructions
Some of the instrumental parts contain special instructions at the end.

Organising your resources

Three different instrumental parts can be played on one instrument by three friendly children. (It may be helpful to encourage children who find this activity easy to share instruments with those who find it harder.)

With more instruments, you can duplicate or use the parts in any way you like to suit your resources. Each part should be played on adjacent notes, which can be high or low.

To help a child see and accurately strike the note-bars of his/her instrumental part, you can remove the adjacent note-bars on either side. For instance, to help a child playing the 1st part of *John Brown's brother*, remove the note **C** on the left of **D**, and **G** on the right of **F**. If children are sharing instruments, this may not be possible as these notes might be required for other parts. In this case, you can mark the notes to be played with coloured stickers – one colour for the note-bars of one instrumental part.

Adding recorders to your performance
Any of the instrumental parts given can be played on recorders – even very elementary pupils may know all the notes required for one of the instrumental parts. Some of the melodies of the songs given on pages 60-63 are in the range of the recorder – these may be appropriate for advanced players.

Verse

What shall we play in our music lesson?

What shall we play in our music lesson?

What shall we play in our music lesson?

Glockenspiels and chime bars.

Chorus

Drums, tambourines and wood blocks,

Drums, tambourines and wood blocks,

Drums, tambourines and wood blocks,

Glockenspiels and chime bars.

This is sung to the tune of *Drunken Sailor*. The children play a chord accompaniment made up of three parts. Each chord is played on the 1st beat – the strong beat.

You will need:
• these notes for the 1st part

• these notes for the 2nd part

• these notes for the 3rd part

• photocopies of the instrumental parts shown opposite
• (optional) any untuned percussion instruments.

		A	A	A	A	A	A	A	D	F	A
		What	shall	we	play	in	our	mu	- sic	les	- son?
1	2	①			2			①		2	
1st part		A						A			
2nd part		F						F			
3rd part		D						D			

What shall we play? – chord accompaniment

1. Count the beat and perform this action pattern with the song.

Divide the children into two groups. One group sings while the other counts the beat 1, 2 throughout, clapping on the 1st beats and moving hands apart on the 2nd beats.

1   2

2. Sing the song several times. On the 1st beats:

• *Read an instrumental part.*
Read one line at a time and point to each note name on the instrumental part.

• *Lightly touch the note-bars.*
Touch the notes indicated on the instrumental part.

• *Play an instrumental part.*
With a beater, strike the note-bars indicated on the instrumental part.

At each of these stages, lift the hand on the 2nd beat, being sure not to make any sound.

3. Perform the song with the chord accompaniment.
Perform two or three of the instrumental parts simultaneously. (If you wish, add untuned percussion to your performance.)

What shall we play?
1st part (G A)

Count 1 2 throughout
Play on ① (the 1st beats)

①	①
A	A
G	G
A	A
G	A

Play twice; once for the verse and once for the chorus.

What shall we play?
2nd part (E F)

Count 1 2 throughout
Play on ① (the 1st beats)

①	①
F	F
E	E
F	F
E	F

Play twice; once for the verse and once for the chorus.

What shall we play?
3rd part (C D)

Count 1 2 throughout
Play on ① (the 1st beats)

①	①
D	D
C	C
D	D
C	D

Play twice; once for the verse and once for the chorus.

This material is photocopiable for the teaching purposes specified in this book.

Verse

John Brown's brother ran from here to Timbuctu,

John Brown's brother ran from here to Timbuctu,

John Brown's brother ran from here to Timbuctu,

He's the fastest man alive!

Chorus

Running round the earth's equator,

Rang to say he'd be home later,

What a speedy operator,

He's the fastest man alive!

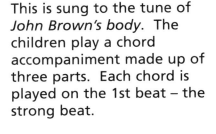

This is sung to the tune of *John Brown's body*. The children play a chord accompaniment made up of three parts. Each chord is played on the 1st beat – the strong beat.

You will need:
- these notes for the 1st part

- these notes for the 2nd part

- these notes for the 3rd part

- photocopies of the instrumental parts shown opposite.

		D	D	B♭	D	G	A	B	B	B	A	G
		John	Brown's	bro-ther	ran	from	here	to	Tim	- buc	-tu	
1	2	①	2	①	2		①	2		①	2	
1st part		D		D			D			D		
2nd part		B		B			B			B		
3rd part		G		G			G			G		

John Brown's brother chord accompaniment

1. Count the beat and perform an action pattern with the song.

Divide the children into two groups; one sings while the other counts the beat 1, 2 throughout, clapping on the 1st beats and moving hands apart on the 2nd beats.

2. Sing the song several times. On the 1st beats:

• **Read an instrumental part.**
   Read one line at a time and point to each note name in turn.

• **Lightly touch the note-bars.**
   Touch the notes indicated on the instrumental part.

• **Play an instrumental part.**
   With a beater, strike the note-bars indicated on the instrumental part.

At each of these stages, lift the hand on the 2nd beat, being sure not to make any sound.

3. Perform the song with the chord accompaniment.
Perform two or three of the instrumental parts simultaneously.

John Brown's brother

1st part (D E F♯)

Count 1 2 throughout
Play on ① (the 1st beats)

①	①	①	①
D	D	D	D
E	E	D	D
D	D	F♯	E
E	F♯	D	D

Play twice; once for the verse and once for the chorus.

John Brown's brother

2nd part (B C D)

Count 1 2 throughout
Play on ① (the 1st beats)

①	①	①	①
B	B	B	B
C	C	B	B
B	B	B	B
C	D	B	B

Play twice; once for the verse and once for the chorus.

John Brown's brother

3rd part (G A)

Count 1 2 throughout
Play on ① (the 1st beats)

①	①	①	①
G	G	G	G
G	G	G	G
G	G	A	G
A	A	G	G

Play twice; once for the verse and once for the chorus.

This material is photocopiable for the teaching purposes specified in this book.

Down by the bay (Down by the bay)

Where the watermelons grow, (Where the watermelons grow)

Back to my home (Back to my home)

I dare not go, (I dare not go)

For if I do (For if I do)

My mother will say: (My mother will say)

"Did you ever see a cow with a green eyebrow

Down by the bay." (Down by the bay)

With this echo song, the children play a chord accompaniment made up of three parts. Each chord is played on the 1st beat – the strong beat.

You will need:
• photocopies of the instrumental parts shown opposite

• these notes for the 1st part

• these notes for the 2nd part

• these notes for the 3rd part.

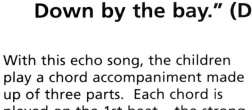

1	2	3	4	1	D	E	D	F#	(F#	F#	F#	F#)
					Down	by	the	bay,	(Down	by	the	bay)
					2	3	4	①	2	3	4	①
1st part								D				D
2nd part								A				A
3rd part								F#				F#

Down by the bay **chord accompaniment**

1. Count the beat and perform an action pattern with the song.

Divide the children into two groups; one sings while the other counts the beat 1, 2, 3, 4 throughout, clapping on the 1st beats and moving hands apart on the 2nd, 3rd and 4th beats.

Notice that the tune of this song begins on the 2nd beat. This means that there are three beats of the tune before the 1st '1st' beat of the song.

```
 2    3    4    1    2    3    4    1
Down  by   the  bay, (Down by   the  bay)
```

2. Sing the song several times. On the 1st beats:

• ***Read an instrumental part.***
  Read one line at a time and point to each note name in turn.

• ***Lightly touch the note-bars.***
  Touch the notes indicated on the instrumental part.

• ***Play an instrumental part.***
  With a beater, strike the note-bars indicated on the instrumental part.

3. Perform the song with the chord accompaniment.
Perform two or three of the instrumental parts simultaneously.

# Down by the bay			
1st part (C D)			
Count 1 2 3 4 throughout **Play on ① (the first beats)**			
①	①	①	①
D	D	D	D
D	D	D	D
C	C	D	D
D	D	D	D

# Down by the bay			
2nd part (G A B)			
Count 1 2 3 4 throughout **Play on ① (the first beats)**			
①	①	①	①
A	A	B	B
A	A	B	B
G	G	B	B
B	A	B	B

# Down by the bay			
3rd part (E F♯ G)			
Count 1 2 3 4 throughout **Play on ① (the 1st beats)**			
①	①	①	①
F♯	F♯	G	G
F♯	F♯	G	G
E	E	G	G
G	F♯	G	G

This material is photocopiable for the teaching purposes specified in this book.

Verse

My penguin has gone to the circus,

My crocodile's gone out to tea,

My elephant's gone to the seaside

And so have my ant and my flea.

Chorus

Bring back, bring back,

Oh, bring back my creatures to me, to me.

Bring back, bring back,

Oh, bring back my creatures to me.

This is sung to the tune of *My bonnie lies over the ocean*. The children play a chord accompaniment made up of three parts. Each chord is played on the 1st beat – the strong beat.

You will need:
• these notes for the 1st part

• these notes for the 2nd part

• these notes for the 3rd part

• photocopies of the instrumental parts shown opposite.

					D	B		A	G	A	G	E	D	B,		
					My	pen	- guin has	gone	to	the	cir	-	cus_____			
1	2	3	1	2	3	①	2	3	①	2	3	①	2	3	①	2
1st part						B			C			B			B	
2nd part						G			G			G			G	
3rd part						D			E			D			D	

My penguin chord accompaniment

1. Count the beat and perform an action pattern with the song.

Divide the children into two groups; one sings while the other counts the beat 1, 2, 3 throughout, clapping on the 1st beats and moving hands apart on the 2nd and 3rd beats.

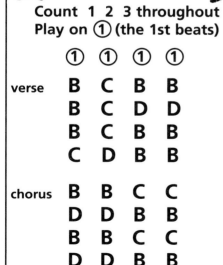

Notice that the tune begins on the beat before the 1st beat. This is called the upbeat.

```
3   1   2   3   1   2
My  pen-guin has gone to ...
```

2. Sing the song several times. On the 1st beats:

• **Read an instrumental part.**
Read one line at a time and point to each note name in turn.

• **Lightly touch the note-bars.**
Touch the notes indicated on the instrumental part.

• **Play an instrumental part.**
With a beater, strike the note-bars indicated on the instrumental part.

3. Perform the song with the chord accompaniment.

Perform two or three of the instrumental parts simultaneously.

 My penguin
1st part (B C D)

Count 1 2 3 throughout
Play on ① (the 1st beats)

	①	①	①	①
verse	B	C	B	B
	B	C	D	D
	B	C	B	B
	C	D	B	B
chorus	B	B	C	C
	D	D	B	B
	B	B	C	C
	D	D	B	B

 My penguin
2nd part (G A)

Count 1 2 3 throughout
Play on ① (the 1st beats)

	①	①	①	①
verse	G	G	G	G
	G	A	A	A
	G	G	G	G
	A	A	G	G
chorus	G	G	G	G
	A	A	G	G
	G	G	G	G
	A	A	G	G

 My penguin
3rd part (D E F#)

Count 1 2 3 throughout
Play on ① (the 1st beats)

	①	①	①	①
verse	D	E	D	D
	D	E	F#	F#
	D	E	D	D
	E	F#	D	D
chorus	D	D	E	E
	F#	F#	D	D
	D	D	E	E
	F#	F#	D	D

Daisy, Daisy,

Give me your answer, do!

I'm half crazy,

All for the love of you!

It won't be a stylish marriage,

I can't afford a carriage,

But you'll look sweet upon the seat

Of a bicycle made for two!

The children play a chord accompaniment made up of three parts. Each chord is played on the 1st beat – the strong beat.

You will need:
• these notes for the 1st part

• these notes for the 2nd part

• these notes for the 3rd part

• photocopies of the instrumental parts shown opposite.

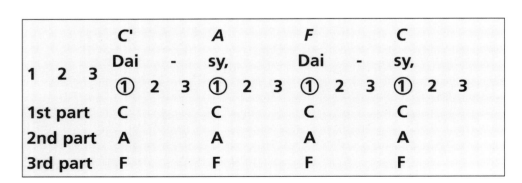

			C'			A			F			C		
			Dai	-	sy,				Dai	-	sy,			
1	2	3	①	2	3	①	2	3	①	2	3	①	2	3
1st part			C			C			C			C		
2nd part			A			A			A			A		
3rd part			F			F			F			F		

Daisy Bell chord accompaniment

1. Count the beat and perform an action pattern with the song.

Divide the children into two groups; one sings while the other counts the beat 1, 2, 3 throughout, clapping on the 1st beats and moving hands apart on the 2nd and 3rd beats.

2. Sing the song several times. On the 1st beats:
• Read an instrumental part.

Read one line at a time and point to each note name in turn.

• **Lightly touch the note-bars.**
Touch the notes indicated on the instrumental part.

• **Play an instrumental part.**
With a beater, strike the note-bars indicated on the instrumental part.

3. Perform the song with the chord accompaniment.
Perform two or three of the instrumental parts simultaneously.

Daisy Bell
1st part (C D E)

Count 1 2 3 throughout
Play on ① (the first beats)

①	①	①	①
C	C	C	C
D	D	C	C
D	E	C	D
D	D	E	E
E	E	C	C
D	D	E	E
C	E	C	E
C	E	C	C

Daisy Bell
2nd part (A B♭ B C)

Count 1 2 3 throughout
Play on ① (the 1st beats)

①	①	①	①
A	A	A	A
B♭	B♭	A	A
B♭	C	A	A
B	B	C	C
C	C	A	A
B♭	B♭	C	C
A	C	A	C
A	C	A	A

Daisy Bell
3rd part (F G)

Count 1 2 3 throughout
Play on ① (the 1st beats)

①	①	①	①
F	F	F	F
F	F	F	F
G	G	F	F
G	G	G	G
G	G	F	F
F	G	G	G
F	G	F	G
F	G	F	F

This material is photocopiable for the teaching purposes specified in this book.

Verse

Carry me ackie, go a Linstead Market,

Not a quattie would sell.

Carry me ackie, go a Linstead Market,

Not a quattie would sell.

Chorus

Lord, not a mite, not a bite,

What a Saturday night!

Lord, not a mite, not a bite

What a Saturday night!

The children play a chord accompaniment made up of three parts. The chords are played on the 1st and 3rd beats.

You will need:
- these notes for the 1st part

- these notes for the 2nd part

- these notes for the 3rd part

- photocopies of the instrumental parts shown opposite.

				A	A	A	F#	A	D'	C#'	B	B	A	A
				Car-ry	me	ack	-	ie, go	a	Lin	- stead	Mar	-	ket,
1	2	3	4	①		2		③	4	①	2	③		4
1st part				A				A		B		A		
2nd part				F#				F#		G		F#		
3rd part				D				D		D		D		

Linstead Market chord accompaniment

1. Count the beat and perform an action pattern with the song.

Divide the children into two groups; one sings while the other counts the beat 1, 2, 3, 4 throughout, clapping on the 1st and 3rd beats and moving hands apart on the 2nd and 4th beats.

2. Sing the song several times. On the 1st beats and 3rd beats:

- **Read an instrumental part.**
  Read one line at a time and point to each note name in turn.
- **Lightly touch the note-bars.**
  Touch the notes indicated on the instrumental part.
- **Play an instrumental part.**
  With a beater, strike the note-bars indicated on the instrumental part.

3. Perform the song with the chord accompaniment.
Perform two or three of the instrumental parts simultaneously.

Linstead Market

 1st part (G A B)

Count 1 2 3 4 throughout
Play on ① and ③
(the 1st and 3rd beats)

	①	③	①	③
verse	A	A	B	A
	G	G	A	G
	A	A	B	A
	G	G	A	A
chorus	A	A	G	A
	G	G	A	G
	A	A	G	A
	G	G	A	A

Linstead Market

 2nd part (F♯ G A)

Count 1 2 3 4 throughout
Play on ① and ③
(the 1st and 3rd beats)

	①	③	①	③
verse	F♯	F♯	G	F♯
	A	A	F♯	A
	F♯	F♯	G	F♯
	A	A	F♯	F♯
chorus	F♯	F♯	A	F♯
	A	A	F♯	A
	F♯	F♯	A	F♯
	A	A	F♯	F♯

Linstead Market

 3rd part (D E)

Count 1 2 3 4 throughout
Play on ① and ③
(the 1st and 3rd beats)

	①	③	①	③
verse	D	D	D	D
	E	E	D	E
	D	D	D	D
	E	E	D	D
chorus	D	D	E	D
	E	E	D	E
	D	D	E	D
	E	E	D	D

Verse

'Tis the gift to be simple, 'tis the gift to be free,

'Tis the gift to come down where you ought to be,

And when we find ourselves in the place just right,

'Twill be in the valley of love and delight.

Chorus

When true simplicity is gained,

To bow and to bend we shan't be ashamed;

To turn, turn will be our delight,

'Til by turning, turning we come round right.

The children play a chord accompaniment made up of three parts. Each chord is played on the 1st and 3rd beats.

You will need:
- these notes for the 1st part
- these notes for the 2nd part
- these notes for the 3rd part

- photocopies of the instrumental parts shown opposite.

			D	D	G		G	A	B	A	B	C'	D'		D'	C'	B
			'Tis	the	gift		to	be	sim-ple,	'tis	the	gift		to	be	free
1	2	3															
			4		①		2		③		4		①		2		③
1st part					D				E				D				E
2nd part					B				B				B				B
3rd part					G				G				F♯				G

Simple gifts chord accompaniment

1. Count the beat and perform an action pattern with the song.

Divide the children into two groups; one sings while the other counts the beat 1, 2, 3, 4 throughout, clapping on the 1st and 3rd beats and moving hands apart on the 2nd and 4th beats.

Notice that the tune begins on the beat before the 1st beat. This is called the upbeat.

4	1	2	3
I	danced	in the	morn-ing...

2. Sing the song several times. On the 1st and 3rd beats:

- **Read an instrumental part.**
  Read one line at a time and point to each note name in turn.
- **Lightly touch the note-bars.**
  Touch the notes indicated on the instrumental part.
- **Play an instrumental part.**
  With a beater, strike the note-bars indicated on the instrumental part.

3. Perform the song with the chord accompaniment.

Perform two or three of the instrumental parts simultaneously.

Simple gifts

1st part (C D E)

Count 1 2 3 4 throughout
Play on ① and ③
(the 1st and 3rd beats)

	①	③	①	③
verse	D	E	D	E
	C	C	C	D
	D	E	D	E
	E	D	D	D
chorus	D	D	E	E
	D	D	C	D
	D	E	D	D
	C	D	D	D

Simple gifts

2nd part (A B C)

Count 1 2 3 4 throughout
Play on ① and ③
(the 1st and 3rd beats)

	①	③	①	③
verse	B	B	B	B
	A	A	A	A
	B	B	B	B
	C	A	B	B
chorus	B	B	B	B
	B	B	A	C
	B	B	B	B
	A	C	B	B

Simple gifts

3rd part (E F♯ G)

Count 1 2 3 4 throughout
Play on ① and ③
(the 1st and 3rd beats)

	①	③	①	③
verse	G	G	F♯	G
	E	E	E	F♯
	G	G	F♯	G
	G	F♯	G	G
chorus	G	G	G	G
	G	F♯	E	F♯
	G	G	G	F♯
	E	F♯	G	G

This material is photocopiable for the teaching purposes specified in this book.

Verse

Alas, my love, you do me wrong,

To cast me off discourteously;

And I have lovéd you so long,

Delighting in your company.

Chorus

Greensleeves was all my joy,

Greensleeves was my delight,

Greensleeves was my heart of gold

And who but my Lady Greensleeves?

With this song, the children play a chord accompaniment made up of three parts. Each chord is played on the 1st and 4th beats.

You will need:
- these notes for the 1st part

- these notes for the 2nd part

- these notes for the 3rd part

- photocopies of the instrumental parts shown opposite.

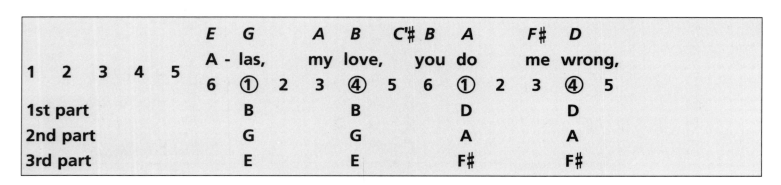

					E	G		A	B	C♯	B	A		F♯	D	
					A - las,			my	love,		you	do		me	wrong,	
1	2	3	4	5	6	①	2	3	④	5	6	①	2	3	④	5
1st part						B			B			D			D	
2nd part						G			G			A			A	
3rd part						E			E			F♯			F♯	

Greensleeves chord accompaniment

1. Count the beat and perform an action pattern with the song.

Divide the children into two groups; one sings while the other counts the beat 1, 2, 3, 4, 5, 6 throughout, clapping on the 1st and 4th beats and moving hands apart on the 2nd, 3rd, 5th and 6th beats.

Notice that the tune begins on the beat before the 1st beat. This is called the upbeat.

```
6   1   2   3   4   5
A - las      my  love ...
```

2. Sing the song several times. On the 1st and 4th beats:

- **Read an instrumental part.**
  Read one line at a time and point to each note name in turn.

- **Lightly touch the note-bars.**
  Touch the notes indicated on the instrumental part.

- **Play an instrumental part.**
  With a beater, strike the note-bars indicated on the instrumental part.

3. Perform the song with the chord accompaniment.
Perform two or three of the instrumental parts simultaneously.

Greensleeves
1st part (B D)
Count 1 2 3 4 5 6 throughout
Play on ① and ④
(the 1st and 4th beats)

	①	④	①	④
verse	B	B	D	D
	B	B	D	D
	B	B	D	D
	B	B	B	B
chorus	D	D	D	D
	B	B	D	D
	D	D	D	D
	B	B	B	B

Greensleeves
2nd part (G A B)
Count 1 2 3 4 5 6 throughout
Play on ① and ④
(the 1st and 4th beats)

	①	④	①	④
verse	G	G	A	A
	G	G	B	B
	G	G	A	A
	G	A	G	G
chorus	B	B	A	A
	G	G	B	B
	B	B	A	A
	G	A	G	G

Greensleeves
3rd part (E F♯ G)
Count 1 2 3 4 5 6 throughout
Play on ① and ④
(the 1st and 4th beats)

	①	④	①	④
verse	E	E	F♯	F♯
	E	E	F♯	F♯
	E	E	F♯	F♯
	E	F♯	E	E
chorus	G	G	F♯	F♯
	E	E	F♯	F♯
	G	G	F♯	F♯
	E	F♯	E	E

Help with composing activities

Composing may sound like a job for the experts, and indeed, if you were given a blank sheet of paper and told to 'make up a piece of music', you might feel at a loss as to where and how to begin. But if you are given a set of boundaries, some guidelines and some rules, the process becomes manageable, and even fun! It follows that if you give your children clear instructions they will enjoy composing their own music.

Discussing composition
Before asking the children to do any composition, consider and discuss with them the tools with which professional composers make their music interesting and effective. These include:
• using the musical elements – pitch, duration, dynamics, tempo, timbre, texture and structure;
• mood and feel (all the elements);
• melody or tune (pitch);
• chords – more than one note at a time (pitch);
• repetition, contrast and the construction and shape of a piece (structure).

Composing activities
Each activity in this section consists of a simple process for the children to go through in order to make up their own music. On the accompanying recording, example pieces of music are given. These are intended to be indications of what might result from going through these processes. Be aware that when making up music, there are no right or wrong ideas, though some may be more effective or more appropriate than others.

Classroom resources and organisation
All the activities in this section can be adapted to suit your resources of instruments and space.

Composing with 9+ year olds
The composing activities in this book require the children to consider several aspects of music at once – unlike composing activities for younger children which often focus on just one musical element, such as dynamics.

Most of the activities in this section require the children to consider musical structure. Activities such as Sounds around (page 44, track 17), The intrepid traveller (page 46, track 18) and Spelling bee (page 48, track 19) suggest structures within which the children adapt their musical ideas. However, activities such as Make a note of your birthday (page 50, track 20) and Whatever the weather (page 56, track 23) require the children to choose ways to organise their ideas. Playing pictures (page 58, track 24) gives the children the opportunity to compare the musical results of different methods of organising sounds.

Both *Sounds around* (page 44, track 17) and *The intrepid traveller* (page 46, track 18) give the opportunity to explore mood and feel. To do this, the children can make use of any musical element – pitch, duration, dynamics, tempo, timbre and texture – to achieve a desired effect. However, *The intrepid traveller* particularly focusses on dynamics.

Spelling bee (page 48, track 19) and *Make a note of your birthday* (page 50, track 20) suggest ways of generating melodies, then incorporating them into pieces of music. To create imaginative pieces of music, the children must find interesting ways to perform their melodies – such as with effective combinations of instruments (texture).

Both *The grand hotel* (page 52, track 21) and *Bookshelves* (page 54, track 22) focus on chords – more than one note played at once. The children explore the sounds of different combinations of notes and evaluate which they like best. They then decide how to perform their chords – choosing tempo, dynamics and so on.

In *Whatever the weather* (page 56, track 23) and *Playing pictures* (page 58, track 24), the children have more freedom to explore mood and feel using structures or processes they choose for themselves. In all of the activities, the children are encouraged to evaluate their own compositions and to find ways of improving them – however, this is particularly important in these last two activities.

Points on performance and appraisal

First and foremost, encourage the children to enjoy their music-making and to develop the means and confidence to perform independently of your help. When they are performing without you, encourage your children to:
• be ready to play;
• begin together at an agreed signal or count in;
• listen carefully to each other.

When appraising your children's performances, commend them not only on content, but on presentation and organisation as well.

Encourage the children to evaluate their own performances. They should actively try to consider how they aim to achieve a musical effect and look for ways to improve upon it.

Above all, try to make the children's experience of composing positive and enjoyable. As with all other creative opportunities, you might be amazed at what they can come up with!

Listen carefully, what can you hear?

Waves lapping, waves lapping.

Listen carefully, what can you hear?

Seagulls calling from the sky.

Listen carefully, what can you hear?

Children splashing in the sea.

Listen carefully, what can you hear?

An ice cream van, an ice cream van.

In this activity, the children make up short pieces of music which represent the sounds of an environment – such as 'by the sea'. The short pieces are then incorporated into a longer piece of music.

You will need:
• as many tuned and untuned percussion instruments as you have available, as well as any additional junk items which might be useful for creating interesting sounds.

1	2	3	4	1	2	3	4	1	2	3	4
				D	D	A	A A B	A	G	A	
				Lis - ten	care - ful - ly, what	can you hear?					

The activity

1. Discuss various environments, and sounds which can be heard in them.
Examples might include the seaside (lapping waves, seagulls calling), the city (engines, road drills, footsteps), and the playground (bouncing balls, teachers talking, children running).

2. Perform a question and answer chant.
The children sit in a circle. Either you, or all the children chant 'Listen carefully, what can you hear?' The children take turns to chant an answer for a chosen environment.

3. The children make up short pieces of music based on their answers in the chant.
Divide the children into groups. Each group chooses an answer as a starting point and makes up a short piece of music. The children decide:
• which instruments to play to suggest their sounds;
• how the instruments should be played to create the right effect;
• how their pieces should be constructed.

4. All of the short pieces are incorporated into a longer piece.
Either you, or everyone now sings the question 'Listen carefully, what can you hear?' to the tune shown opposite. The groups take turns to perform their short piece in answer to the question.

5. The children discuss their short pieces.
They can compare their pieces, evaluate how successful they sound when performed in turn in the longer piece and consider improvements.

In this activity, the children compose music to illustrate the journey of a traveller. Dynamics (loud and quiet sounds) are explored through the changing condition of geographical features – water, a volcano, snow and a tropical storm.

You will need:
• as many tuned and untuned percussion instruments as you have available
• photocopies of the illustration showing the traveller's journey.

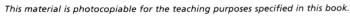

This material is photocopiable for the teaching purposes specified in this book.

The activity

1. Discuss the changing geographical features encountered in the explorer's journey.

Give the children photocopies of the illustrations of the explorer's journey. Discuss how:
• the **water** increases from a stream to an ocean (1-3);
• the **volcano** goes from calm to angry (3-5);
• the **snow** falls and gathers (6-8);
• the **tropical storm** gathers momentum (9-10).

2. Discuss the musical effect of increasing or decreasing volume in music.

The changing geographical features in the explorer's journey can be suggested in music with changing dynamics.

Discuss ways to change dynamics, such as:
• changing the way in which you play an instrument to give a louder or quieter effect;
• increasing or decreasing the number of instruments playing together;
• choosing loud or quiet instruments (a cymbal, played with the same effort as Indian bells, will sound louder);
• any combination of these.

3. The children compose short pieces of music for the geographical features.

Divide the children into four groups and delegate a geographical feature to each. Encourage them to choose appropriate instruments and to use suitable dynamics.

4. The children perform their short pieces of music in order.

They perform in the order shown in the illustration without a pause between sections, making one piece of music depicting the explorer's whole journey.

This material is photocopiable for the teaching purposes specified in this book.

Spelling bee words

2-letter word
BE

3-letter words
ADD ACE AGE BAD BAG BED
BEE BEG CAB DAB DAD EBB EGG
FAB FAD FED FEE GAG

4-letter words
AGED BABE BEAD BEEF CAFE
CAGE CEDE DEAD DEAF DEED
EDGE FACE FADE FEED

5-letter words
ADDED BADGE CADGE CAGED EBBED
EDGED EGGED FACED FADED

6-letter words
ACCEDE BEGGED DABBED DECADE
DEFACE FACADE FAFFED GAGGED

7-letter words
BAGGAGE CABBAGE DEFACED

In this activity, the children choose melodies made by words spelt with letters that are note names.

The children order the melodies according to a musical structure called rondo. In a rondo the first section (called the A section) is repeated after contrasting sections of music (called the B section, C section and so on), making an A B A C A D A structure. (Remember that the letters here are not note names.)

Each group will need:
• at least one instrument with these notes

• beaters
• photocopies of the *Spelling bee words*
• large pieces of paper and pencils.

The activity

1. Divide the children into groups.

Give each a photocopy of the *Spelling bee words*.

2. Each group finds four Spelling bee words which, when played, make pleasing melodies.

Encourage the children to choose words for the sound of the melodies they make, rather than for the literal meaning of the words.

Each group finds ways to perform its melodies – quickly, slowly, with particular rhythms or with sounds played on other percussion instruments.

3. Each group decides which of its melodies should be the 'A' section, the 'B' section and so on of its rondo.

The melody used for the 'A' section should be performed in the same way each time it is repeated. The other sections should contrast with the 'A' section. They might contrast by having:
• a different number of notes in the melody;
• a different starting or ending note;
• a different rhythm;
• a different mode of performance or accompaniment.

4. Each group notates its piece.

Each group finds a way to write down its piece. The words should be written with capital letters and can be illustrated. Any features of the piece that the children feel are important can be represented.

5. Each group performs its piece.

Each group can display its notation at the same time.

A sample rondo composition

BADGE
slow slow quick quick slow

EBB

BADGE
slow slow quick quick slow

CAFE

BADGE
slow slow quick quick slow

DECADE
quick quick quick quick slow slow

BADGE
slow slow quick quick slow

A sample birthday phrase

The composer Wolfgang Amadeus Mozart was born on 27th January 1756. We can write this as 27 01 1756. Translated using the birthday code opposite, his birthday tune would read like this:

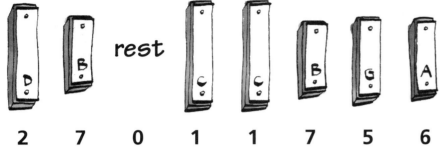

The children use their dates of birth and the birthday code to make short tunes. These are then incorporated and developed into a composition.

You will need:
• instruments containing these notes

• as many untuned percussion instruments as you have available
• photocopies of the *Birthday code* shown opposite
• paper and pencils

A sample plan for a composition

Read one line at a time.
Play at a Moderate speed.
● = tambourine   △ = triangle

Mozart's birthday tune

Bach's birthday tune

Prokofiev's birthday tune

The activity

1. The children work out their birthday tunes.

Each child writes down his or her date of birth in number form, eg 18 08 1988. Everyone's date of birth will contain at least one 9 – which can be any note with a ♯ or ♭ in its name. The children try out their melodies on tuned percussion and decide which note to use for number 9.

2. The children develop compositions out of the birthday tunes.

Divide the children into groups. Each group considers how to organise its birthday tunes into a larger composition. The children may:

• play their tunes one after another, to make one long tune;

• repeat a tune or parts of a tune;

• play two tunes simultaneously;

• use contrasting volume (play loudly or quietly, or in between);

• use contrasting speeds (play quickly or slowly, or in between)

• develop accompaniments for their compositions using untuned percussion instruments of their choice.

3. Each group writes down a plan for its composition.

The children will need to decide what are the main features and characteristics of their pieces, and find appropriate ways of notating them.

4. Each group performs its composition.

Each group can display its plan, explaining what it shows, then perform its composition.

Birthday code

1 = C
2 = D
3 = E
4 = F
5 = G
6 = A
7 = B
8 = C

9 = any note with a ♯ or ♭ in its name

0 = silent rest

This material is photocopiable for the teaching purposes specified in this book.

In this activity, the children are divided into pairs to make up tunes which are seven notes long. Each note is written in a window of each top floor room of the *grand hotel*. The children then find seven lower notes for the ground floor which sound well when played simultaneously with the top floor.

Each pair of children will need:
• at least one tuned instrument with these notes

• at least two beaters
• a photocopy of the empty *grand hotel*
• a pencil.

This material is photocopiable for the teaching purposes specified in this book.

The activity

1. Divide the children into pairs.
Allocate instruments, photocopies of the hotel and pencils.

2. Each pair makes up a tune.
The tune should be seven notes long. Starting in the top left window, the children write the name of each note in the seven windows. (If they wish, they can choose names beginning with each letter and fill those in, thus naming the seven guests on the top floor.)

3. The children find seven lower notes which sound well when played with the notes of the tune.
The children write the note-names in the ground floor rooms. (Again, if they wish, they can choose names beginning with each letter, thus naming the seven ground floor guests.)

4. Each pair performs and evaluates its piece based on its guest list.
The children might like to play both floors of the hotel simultaneously – or to play the top floor first, then the ground floor, then both floors simultaneously.

The children evaluate their piece and explore changes that might improve it – such as substituting a note or changing the way in which the piece is performed.

Book title:

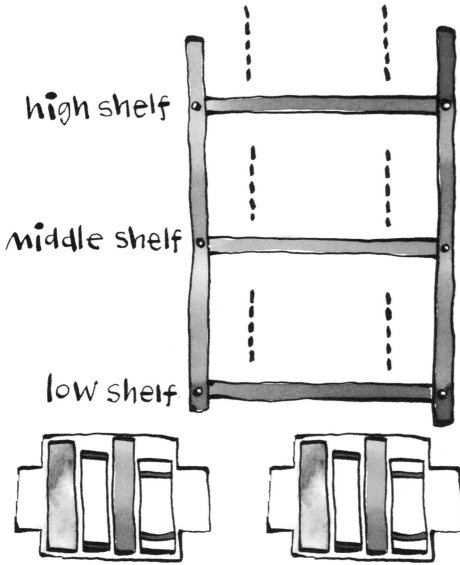

high shelf

middle shelf

low shelf

A group of notes played simultaneously is called a chord. In this activity, children make up four chords – each consisting of three notes which, when played together, sound pleasing.

The children write their notes on books to go on the high, middle, and low shelves of a bookcase. The highest note of each chord is written on books to go on the high shelf, the middle notes go on the middle shelf and low notes go on the low shelf. The chords are then performed to the rhythm of a chosen book title.

For each group, you will need:
• one tuned instrument and three beaters
• three photocopied rows of books
• a photocopy of the empty bookshelf, cut along the dotted lines so that the rows of books can slot in
• pencils and a ruler.

This material is photocopiable for the teaching purposes specified in this book.

The activity

1. Prepare for the activity.

Divide the children into groups of four. Three children are allocated one shelf each and the fourth child is the librarian (and conductor). Make sure that the photocopiable bookcase has been cut along the dotted lines so that the three rows of books can be slotted in. Each group chooses the name of a book to write in the title space above the bookcase.

2. The children choose notes for four chords.

The children work together to find good combinations of notes for each chord. Some combinations will sound more pleasing than others. When the children find three notes which sound well together, they write them down on a vertical column of books on the shelves – the highest note on the high shelf, the middle note on the middle shelf and the low note on the lowest shelf.

When the children have found and written down notes for four chords, they remove the rows of books to leave an empty bookcase – ready for the next stage.

3. The librarian chooses a speed at which the rhythm of the book's title will be played.

(S)he might choose: very fast, quite fast, quite slow or very slow. (S)he may use one speed throughout a whole performance, or several different speeds.

4. The librarian conducts a performance.

The librarian announces the book title. Then (s)he chooses any row of books, and slots it into its shelf on the bookcase. Always reading from left to right, (s)he points with a ruler to the four books in turn, indicating when the performer should play the rhythm of the book title on each note. (S)he adds a second row of books and, holding the ruler vertically, conducts two players at once. Finally, the third row is added and all three players perform simultaneously.

5. Each group evaluates its piece.

If they wish, the children can experiment with ways to improve their piece, perhaps by changing a chord, the order of the chords, the order in which the players perform, or the speed of the performance.

Book title:
Alice in Wonderland

Weather

In this activity, the children make up short sections of music suggested by weather – rain, sun, wind and so on. They then devise weather sequences to order or structure the musical ideas.

You will need:
• as many tuned and untuned percussion instruments as you can make available.

A sample weather sequence

snow wind snow   rain & sun, rainbow   snow wind snow

The activity

1. Discuss weather.
The children can list different kinds of weather.

2. The children make up short sections of weather music.
Divide the children into groups. Each group makes a selection of weather types and, for each, it makes up a short section of music. Allow the children to choose from various instruments in order to create sounds suggested by the various types of weather.

3. The short sections of weather music are ordered according to weather sequences.
Each group thinks of a weather sequence and orders its short sections of music according to it.

Some weather sequences may produce more effective pieces of music than others. Allow the children time to experiment with different weather sequences and to choose the one they feel makes the most effective piece of music.

4. Each group performs a piece of music based on its chosen weather sequence.
If you wish, the rest of the class can try to work out the weather sequence of each piece by listening.

Variations
- The children can code their weather sequences using the letters A, B, C, D and so on. (A stands for the first weather and its repetitions, B for the second and its repetitions and so on.)

A sample composition plan

snow wind snow rain&sun, rainbow snow wind snow

In this activity, the children make up music using sounds suggested by a picture.

You will need:
• as many tuned and untuned instruments you have available
• enlarged photocopies of the pictures, and if you wish, as varied a collection of pictures from as wide a range of sources as you like. Postcards, photographs, magazines, newspapers, books, cartoons and catalogues are all possible sources of pictures.

This material is photocopiable for the teaching purposes specified in this book.

The activity

1. Divide the children into small groups.
Each group chooses, or is allocated, a picture.

2. The children find sounds suggested by their picture.
Sounds can be suggested by any aspect of a picture:
• the subject, features or background;
• style (and colours);
• a suggested event;
• mood.

Some pictures may suggest obvious sounds, whereas others may require more imagination. Praise imaginative ideas and allow subjective opinions to be valid.

3. The children explore three ways to organise their sounds into compositions.
Each group tries all of the following approaches:
• To cue sounds, a conductor might point one by one to elements on the picture which suggest sounds.
• To cue the beginning and ends of sounds, a conductor can move a ruler vertically from left to right across the picture.
• Sounds can be ordered according to an agreed sequence of events suggested by the picture.

4. Each group evaluates and compares its resulting compositions.
They might like to decide which one they like best and why.

This material is photocopiable for the teaching purposes specified in this book.

Melody lines

What shall we play? - Drunken Sailor

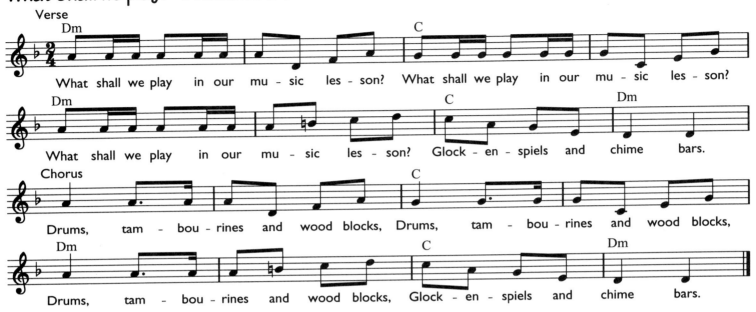

John Brown's brother - John Brown's baby

Melody lines

My penguin - *My bonnie lies over the ocean*   **Page 32, Track 12**

Melody lines

Daisy Bell

Page 34, Track 13

Dai - sy, Dai - sy, Give me your ans - wer, do! _____

I'm half cra - zy All for the love of you! _____ It

won't be a sty - lish mar - riage, _____ I can't af - ford a car - riage, _____ But

you'll look sweet u - pon the seat of a bi - cy - cle made for two! _____

Linstead market

Page 36, Track 14

Verse

Car - ry me ack - ie, go a Lin - stead Mar - ket, Not a quat - tie would sell.

Car - ry me ack - ie, go a Lin - stead Mar - ket, Not a quat - tie would sell.

Chorus

Lord, not a mite, not a bite, What a Sa - tur - day night!

Lord, not a mite, not a bite, What a Sa - tur - day night!

62

Melody lines

Simple gifts

Page 38, Track 15

Verse

'Tis the gift to be sim-ple, 'tis the gift to be free, 'Tis the gift to come down where you ought to be, And

when we find our-selves in the place just __ right, 'Twill be in the val-ley of love and de-light.

Chorus

When true sim-pli-ci-ty is gained, To bow and to bend we __ shan't be a-shamed; To

turn, turn will be our de-light, 'Til by turn-ing, turn-ing we come round right.

Greensleeves

Page 40, Track 16

Verse

A - las, my love, __ you do me wrong, __ To cast me off __ dis - cour - teous - ly; And

I have lo - véd you so long, __ De - light - ing in __ your com - pa - ny.

Chorus

Green - sleeves __ was all my joy, __ Green - sleeves __ was my de - light,

Green sleeves was my heart of gold __ And who but my La - dy Green - sleeves?

Index and glossary

Accidental
A note with a *flat* or *sharp* in its name, eg. **B♭**, **G♯**.

Accompaniment
Music which supports the main instrumental or vocal line, e.g. the piano music or percussion part which is played while someone sings a song.

Chord
A group of two or more notes played together.

Duration
Long and short sounds, pulse, beat and *rhythm*.

Dynamics
Loud and quiet sounds, and silence.

Flat
The musical sign ♭; it lowers the note it refers to by a *semitone*. When flattened, **E** is lowered to **E♭**.

Interval
The distance in sound between two notes.

Major and minor
Both describe types of *intervals, scales* and *chords*. Two notes a 'major 3rd' *(interval)* apart are four *semitones* apart; two notes a 'minor 3rd' apart are three *semitones* apart. A major *scale* contains a major 3rd between its 1st and 3rd notes, whereas a minor *scale* contains a minor 3rd between its 1st and 3rd notes. A major *chord* consists of the 1st, 3rd and 5th notes of a major *scale*, whereas a minor *chord* consists of the 1st, 3rd and 5th notes of a minor *scale*.

Pitch
High and low sounds, and in between.

Rest
A silence, or moment during which a performer does not perform. It can be of specific duration.

Rhythm
The grouping of short and long sounds, and silences.

Rondo
A musical *structure*. The first section (A) is repeated after contrasting sections (B, C, D and so on) making an A B A C A D A structure.

Scale
A succession of rising or falling notes.

Semitone
The smallest interval in Western music; it is the distance between two adjacent notes on a piano keyboard.

Sharp
The musical sign ♯; it raises the note it refers to by a *semitone*. When sharpened, **C** is raised to **C♯**.

Structure
Sections of music and repetition.

Tempo
Fast and slow, and in between.

Texture
One sound performed on its own, or more than one sound played or sung at the same time.

Timbre
The quality of a sound.

The author and publishers would like to thank the following copyright holders and contributors:

Carrie Morrow for the original ideas from which **Sort out the sounds** and **Pieces of eight** were developed © 1996 Carrie Morrow.

For their help in the preparation of this book the author and publishers would like to thank Rosie Cooke, Lynne Jackson, Theresa Kelly, Tracey Lumsden, Sheena Roberts and Allan Watson.